THE NOTIFICATION

by Brandon Haywood

Table of Contents

THE NOTIFICATION

Chapter 1: The Ping

The sound pierced Jasmine Brooks' sleep—high-pitched, sharp, and wrong.

She bolted upright in bed, heart hammering. The room was dark, save for the dim glow o her phone screen beside her. She reached for it instinctively, her fingers trembling slightly One notification glared up at her in bold red text:

"You're being watched."

No app name. No sender. Just that.

She stared at it. The icon was unfamiliar—an obsidian circle with a crimson iris at its cent It pulsed once, like a heartbeat. Then it disappeared. Gone. Not archived. Not dismissed.

Vanished.

Jasmine sat frozen, the cold sweat already forming along her collarbone. Her room was si except for the hum of her ceiling fan. Her phone now looked completely normal—no ale no logs, no recent notifications.

It should've been a dream. It felt like one. But after six years in cybersecurity, Jasmine hac learned the hard way—there's no such thing as coincidence in tech. Especially not in Atlanta, where the city's heartbeat ran on fiber and Wi-Fi.

She pulled up her diagnostics, checking system activity. No recent app launches. No background processes out of place. No files accessed.

It made no sense.

Unless someone had bypassed her security.

Unless someone had found a backdoor she didn't know existed.

She swung her legs over the bed and walked barefoot to the kitchen, the hardwood cool beneath her feet. Outside her apartment, the city stirred. A siren howled in the distance.

sic drifted up from a car idling at a stoplight. But none of it touched her now. She poured ass of water, staring out the window at nothing.

ɔu're being watched."

ɛ words echoed again, heavy in her mind. She ran her hand through her curls and exhaled. r life wasn't exactly high-profile. She freelanced for security firms, taught coding rkshops on the side, and kept to herself. She didn't stir things up. Not recently.

: she had built something once—something powerful. Something anonymous. Privacy tware designed to block facial recognition and metadata tracking. She and her friend Maya l released it under a public license, open-source. A passion project.

d then Maya had disappeared.

at was almost a year ago.

nine took another sip of water and tapped the side of the glass. Her instincts were eaming.

nething was starting.

d this message—it wasn't just a warning.

vas the first move.

Chapter 2: Digital Footprint

By morning, Jasmine's apartment had transformed into a digital crime lab.

Her laptop sat open on the counter, running simultaneous scans through multiple firewa A backup phone buzzed on airplane mode, ready for controlled testing. She'd already pu her main phone apart, laid its motherboard bare under the glare of a magnifying lamp. N loose circuits. No rogue chips. No signs of tampering.

And yet, the message had returned.

"You're being watched."

Same font. Same icon. Same chill that crawled down her spine.

Jasmine stood in her kitchen, one hand gripping the edge of the sink. Her reflection in th microwave door stared back at her, exhausted but razor-focused. She'd wiped devices before—clean slates, factory resets, even magnetic degaussing once when a client suspec NSA-grade implants. But this? This felt more intimate. Like someone was watching her breathe.

She turned to her laptop and dove deeper.

Command-line diagnostics. System log combs. Root access pathways.

The software architecture had no red flags. Not a single unusual signature. But that was t problem—whoever had done this knew how to hide beneath the surface. No traditional malware. No packet leaks. Whoever was behind it had bypassed conventional exploits. T weren't invading her system.

They were already inside.

She paused, staring at the screen, heart racing. This wasn't a script kiddie. This was custo code. Precision-built.

She reached for her second phone and dialed the only person who might believe her.

Trey picked up on the second ring. "It's early. You good?"

"No," she said. "Something's in my system. It's not logging. It's not traceable. It sent me message—twice."

"What kind of message?"

She hesitated. "It said… I'm being watched."

ere was silence on the other end.

nat's not malware," Trey said finally. "Could be ghost protocol. Something modular. note-deployable. You got anything that would make you a target?"

mine rubbed her temples. "Remember that privacy suite I worked on with Maya? The one t blocked facial recognition?"

ne one that went viral in niche corners of GitHub? Yeah. Why?"

aya's name came up. In the message."

y's tone shifted. "I thought she ghosted."

ne didn't. She disappeared."

other silence.

n coming over," he said. "Don't touch anything else."

mine ended the call and locked her screen.

walked slowly toward her living room window and peered between the blinds.

ross the street, a man in a dark hoodie stood by a lamppost. Still. Too still.

d staring directly at her window.

Chapter 3: Ghost in the Machine

Trey arrived just after dusk, carrying a matte-black backpack filled with tools. No greetin no banter. He moved with the calm urgency of someone who'd seen too much.

"Start from the top," he said as he set up his rig on Jasmine's kitchen table.

She recapped the events—the notification, the disappearing app icon, the impossible diagnostics. When she mentioned Maya's name, Trey's eyes darkened. "You didn't tell m her name showed up in the message."

"I wasn't sure it mattered."

"It does. A lot."

He opened his case and began unpacking a compact, custom-built diagnostic tower—hardened firmware, untraceable OS, completely air-gapped. As the machine booted, he connected Jasmine's stripped-down phone to the analyzer port.

"Let's see what the ghost left behind."

Lines of code flew across the screen. Trey narrowed his eyes. "Okay. This is bad."

"How bad?" Jasmine asked.

"This code isn't just encrypted—it's modular. It adapts. There's no fixed footprint. It evolves every time it launches. Like it's learning your system and rewriting itself to hide better."

She stepped closer. "So it's alive?"

"Not in the sci-fi way," he said, "but close. Someone built this thing to survive inside hos environments. No logs, no storage, no tracebacks. It exists in pulses—short bursts of activity, then vanishes like it was never there."

He leaned in, tapping into a subroutine.

"Jas, this isn't malware. It's a surveillance tool. A highly sophisticated one. Military or corporate-grade. Maybe even something darker."

"Why me?"

He looked at her. "Because you built the one thing it's trying to kill—privacy."

The air in the room felt heavier.

en, the phone buzzed again.

th of them froze.

e screen lit up. The same message:

ou're being watched."

t this time, it didn't vanish right away. A second line blinked beneath it:

aya tried to run."

mine stared at the words. Her throat went dry.

ie didn't ghost," she whispered. "She was hunted."

y checked the console. "Something's piggybacking. A deeper function. Wait—there's a load embedded in the notification protocol… I'm decrypting it."

noment later, the screen filled with cascading names. A list.

scrolled.

ya's name appeared. Jasmine's followed three entries down.

iis isn't just a tracking tool," Trey muttered. "It's a targeting system."

mine backed away from the screen, her heart thudding in her chest. "A hit list."

nd you're next."

Chapter 4: The First Vanishing

The drive across Atlanta felt longer than it should have.

Jasmine gripped the steering wheel tighter as the city morphed around her—bright intersections fading into cracked sidewalks and shuttered corner stores. She hadn't been Maya's old place in almost a year. Not since the day Maya went completely dark.

She pulled into the lot behind the Edgewood apartment complex. It hadn't changed. Sam graffiti-tagged dumpster. Same broken security light flickering like a dying pulse. The stai creaked as she climbed to the second floor. She hesitated at the door to Unit 2B, then knocked.

Silence.

She knocked again, louder. "Maya?"

No answer.

She tried the knob—locked. Peering through the window, she saw the apartment in disar A few half-packed boxes. A kitchen chair overturned. Thick layers of dust clung to everything, undisturbed. No signs of recent life.

But it didn't feel like someone had moved out. It felt like someone had been erased.

Jasmine turned and walked down the hall to the landlord's office. The building manager, older man with nicotine-stained fingers and the attention span of a houseplant, barely glanced up when she asked about Maya.

"Left in a rush," he said. "Didn't leave a number. Just dropped the keys in the mail slot. Place has been empty since."

"No one came looking for her?"

"Just you," he muttered. "Now if you're not taking the unit—"

Jasmine left before he finished the sentence.

Back upstairs, she lingered outside Maya's door. Her eyes scanned the floor. Something caught her attention near the welcome mat—one corner slightly raised. She knelt and lift it.

There, carved faintly into the floorboard beneath, were four words etched by hand:

HEY MADE ME DISAPPEAR."

e message was shallow, almost missed under the dust. Jasmine stared at it, her chest ntening.

ya hadn't run.

'd tried to warn someone. Anyone.

mine pulled out her phone, hands shaking. She called Trey.

answered instantly. "Talk to me."

ne didn't leave. She was taken."

believe it," he said. "Because I just ran a deeper crack through the toolset. That payload m earlier? It's a kill chain. A full execution protocol. Flagged individuals get scrubbed— itally and physically."

mine closed her eyes. "She was number one on the list."

ou're number four," Trey said. "And the top three are already inactive."

mine rose to her feet slowly. The message on the floorboard felt like a final whisper— ya's last breath encoded in wood and fear.

ne knew it was coming," Jasmine whispered. "And no one stopped it."

ey was quiet for a beat. "Then we will."

e stepped back, leaving the mat slightly lifted—like an unspoken promise to come back d finish what Maya started.

cause this wasn't just a mystery anymore.

was a countdown.

Chapter 5: Red Lines

Jasmine didn't sleep that night.

Every noise outside her apartment—every siren, every passing engine—felt like a signal. blinds stayed shut, and her lights off. But she knew it didn't matter. The threat wasn't jus outside.

It was already inside everything.

By the second day, she noticed the patterns. A black SUV parked across the street. Same time every morning. Tinted windows. Engine off. Sometimes the driver stayed inside. Ot times, the vehicle sat empty, waiting.

Her building's concierge casually mentioned someone asking about her apartment—clair to be an old college friend. Gave a different name than what she'd used at Georgia Tech.

At her usual coffee shop, a new barista appeared. He didn't make eye contact, didn't smil Just slid her drink across the counter and held her gaze too long when she turned to leav

The city had started breathing on her neck.

She ran a secure wipe on all her devices. Deleted personal backups, encrypted what she needed, burned everything else. Her smartwatch began vibrating at odd intervals. Ghost notifications with no source.

Even her laptop, which she had scrubbed three times, refused to shut down on comman

Trey called her in a rush. "Power down. Hard kill on all electronics. I think the system's escalated."

"What do you mean?" she asked, even though she already knew.

"I tracked the ghost protocol's last beacon," he said. "It pinged your GPS five minutes ag Jasmine—they're watching in real time."

She ended the call and ripped her router from the wall.

That afternoon, Trey didn't answer her messages.

She went to his place.

His front door was open. Slightly. Like someone wanted her to find it.

ide, everything was smashed.

server tower lay on its side, cracked open like a broken vault. Wires spilled across the pet. The apartment was cold, too quiet. A laptop screen flickered in the corner, but all s were wiped. Not just deleted—shredded.

en she found him.

y was slumped against the kitchen counter, blood matting his hair. Conscious, barely. He ked up with one swollen eye.

ney found the backups," he muttered. "Every copy. They knew."

mine crouched beside him, hand trembling as she pressed a towel to his forehead. "Why n't they finish the job?"

coughed. "Because they're warning you."

r eyes darted across the apartment. A yellow sticky note sat near the broken rig. Just three rds:

TOP LOOKING."

mine stared at it, chest rising and falling with tight, shallow breaths. This wasn't paranoia more. This wasn't just about digital shadows.

vas personal.

ou okay?" she whispered to Trey.

didn't answer. Just slid a thumb drive into her palm, slick with his blood. She looked wn. A label scratched into it with a knife:

LAS.

stood slowly.

e line had been drawn.

d she had already crossed it.

Chapter 6: Code Named Atlas

The thumb drive felt like it weighed a thousand pounds.

Jasmine held it between her fingers, staring at the crude carving scratched into its casing: ATLAS. It wasn't a brand. It was a name.

She plugged it into her offline rig—an old laptop she kept air-gapped from every network No cloud sync. No Bluetooth. No Wi-Fi. Just pure, isolated processing.

The contents were encrypted under a triple-shielded cipher. Trey's work. She recognized structuring—three-pass authentication, randomized hash keys, digital deadman timers. It took her the better part of an hour to crack it open.

What she found made her blood run cold.

Inside was a collection of internal memos, logs, and surveillance diagrams. Each file was cleanly formatted, almost clinical in its tone. The documents detailed something called Project Atlas—a predictive AI system originally developed as a joint venture between priv security firms and unnamed government contractors.

The earliest files painted it as a behavioral analysis tool. Something to monitor online chat detect threat patterns, flag potential domestic violence or terror threats.

But the newest files were different.

They outlined protocols for something called Preemptive Elimination. No due process. N intervention.

Just identification. Monitoring. And if the threat level crossed a threshold… deletion.

Digital first. Physical next.

Jasmine scrolled through the list of target parameters—privacy advocates, whistleblowers, anti-surveillance developers. It read like a blacklist of free thinkers. Her name was there. S was Maya's. Even Trey's alias popped up.

The logs included timestamps, social web mapping, facial analysis algorithms. There were full psychological profiles based on digital behavior. One file even speculated on Jasmine's "likelihood of disruption" with a confidence score of 87.6%.

She leaned back from the screen, overwhelmed. "They're not just watching us," she whispered. "They're pruning us."

: transferred the files to a hardened drive, encrypted them, then snapped the original .mb in half. She couldn't afford to leave a trail. Not now.

e final file in the folder was a map.

howed known Atlas nodes—physical server sites across the country. Most were disguised :elecom buildings or abandoned infrastructure. One was marked right outside Atlanta.

catur.

at's where it lived. Where it stored everything.

: called Trey's burner, half-expecting silence. But he picked up, groggy.

ou found it?" he asked.

:oject Atlas. It's real. And it's evolving."

hen it's not about stopping it anymore," he rasped. "It's about exposing it."

: nodded to herself. "We burn it down."

chuckled weakly. "Now you sound like Maya."

mine's eyes flicked to the map.

ood," she said. "Then maybe we have a chance."

Chapter 7: Whistleblower

The message came through an encrypted forum buried five layers deep into the dark-net.

"I helped build it. I can prove it. Meet me. No devices. No names."

It was signed by a handle Trey recognized: deadcircuit47. A name that had popped up in whistleblower communities months ago, claiming to be a former engineer on Atlas's desi team. Most thought it was a troll.

But the detail in the message—specific firmware references, system commands only an insider would know—said otherwise.

They agreed to meet in neutral ground: a 24-hour coin laundromat on Moreland Avenue, where the machines were louder than the city and the cameras had long since stopped working.

Jasmine wore a hoodie, hair tucked beneath a ballcap, and entered at 2:59 AM. The smell bleach and burnt lint filled the air. A single man sat in the far corner near a humming dryer—mid-40s, gaunt, with sunken eyes and nervous fingers that drummed against his th like a metronome.

"You Jasmine?" he asked without looking up.

She hesitated. "You first."

He smirked faintly. "Call me Dylan. I used to be someone important. Now I'm just… someone alive."

He handed her a small USB drive wrapped in electrical tape.

"That's everything I could scrape before I went dark. Footage, logs, test data. Even the command script that activates a wipe on flagged targets. You'll want to verify it all yourse of course."

Jasmine didn't move. "Why are you helping me?"

"Because I built it to stop crimes. Predict disasters. Stop the bad before it happened. But Atlas doesn't wait for proof anymore. It just… assumes. You trip the wrong metric, post wrong article, use the wrong VPN, and boom—flagged. First digitally. Then physically. A no one knows."

He glanced over his shoulder. "Most don't even realize they've been erased until it's too late."

nine's fingers curled around the drive. "How much of Atlanta is a test zone?"

of it," Dylan said. "They've got five cities running quietly. Atlanta was first. They use r traffic cams, your Wi-Fi pings, your water usage. Hell, even your car's GPS. They know re you are more accurately than your mother."

felt the weight of those words. "How do we kill it?"

u don't," he said. "You expose it. Make it undeniable. Make it political poison. They t run it if people won't support it."

stood abruptly. "And one more thing—don't trust anyone with a badge. Some are gged in. Most don't even know. But once Atlas flags you, anyone could be the delivery em."

nine nodded slowly.

an walked past her, hands in his pockets. At the door, he paused and looked back.

ey'll come for you soon. You know that, right?"

n counting on it," she said.

l then he was gone.

nine looked down at the USB in her hand.

truth. One last shot.

Chapter 8: The Data Purge

It started with a denied transaction.

Jasmine tried to buy a sandwich at a corner deli—her debit card declined. She laughed it at first, handed the cashier another. Declined again.

She opened her banking app.

"User credentials not found."

She froze.

Then came the texts from her utilities provider: "Your identity could not be verified." H DMV app wouldn't recognize her license. Her student loans said she'd never existed. He credit score dropped to zero. Her Gmail account locked her out, citing "unusual activity.

She rushed home. Pulled out her backup rig and scanned everything.

What she found was worse than she imagined.

Her name had been scrubbed from every validating database she had ever touched. Publi records, financial ledgers, tax histories, even childhood medical documents—all wiped. T few remaining entries were corrupted or flagged as mismatches.

Trey called her, breathless.

"It's started," he said. "They're deleting you."

Jasmine stared at her own name in an old contact list. BROOKS, JASMINE—grayed ou She couldn't even open the file. "They've got full metadata control?"

"More than that. They're erasing trust anchors. If a system can't verify you, it treats you l a glitch."

She closed her eyes. "They're making it so I don't exist."

Trey's voice was tight. "You've got maybe twenty-four hours before biometric scans flag as fraudulent. Maybe less."

Jasmine went to work.

She dumped every device she owned. Burned SIM cards. Pulled physical drives from old laptops and smashed them with a hammer. She replaced her clothes with thrift shop basi d her hair black. Cut it unevenly. Used a burner mirror to check her reflection. She ı't look like herself anymore—and that was the point.

moved fast, switching to cash, logging into nothing. Her life had to go analog.

before she left, she opened Dylan's USB drive one last time. Inside, a folder titled:

ARDPOINTS/PHYSICAL_NODES/

clicked it.

ɔs. Floorplans. Access logs.

: address was circled—an abandoned AT&T telecom hub on the outskirts of Decatur. ged:

TIVE STORAGE NODE / LOCAL ARCHIVE – PROJECT ATLAS.

stared at it, heart pounding.

tlas lived anywhere—truly lived—it was there.

grabbed a burner phone and tossed it in the dumpster as she left her apartment for the time. Her backpack carried only what she needed to take a system down.

n this point forward, she wasn't Jasmine Brooks anymore.

was just a problem the system hadn't solved yet.

Chapter 9: Backdoor Access

The Decatur hub was a relic—an old AT&T building tucked behind an overgrown parkir lot and rusted-out fencing. The windows were boarded. The sign half-fallen. It looked lik graveyard for forgotten tech.

Which made it the perfect place to hide something powerful.

Jasmine scoped the site from a wooded slope across the road. One guard. No badge. No logo. Just a man with a tactical build and a tired walk, pacing between the side and back entrances every eight minutes. There were cameras—but two were dead and the third rotated just slow enough to offer a blind spot.

At 2:07 AM, she slipped in through a gap in the fence and crouched beside a generator casing. Her pulse was steady. Controlled. She had done this sort of thing before—penetration testing, physical infiltration exercises—but never with her life on the line.

Inside the building, the air was damp and electric. The lights overhead flickered to life on by one, motion-triggered. She moved quickly, stepping over puddles and coiled cable.

Down one dark hallway, she found the core.

Room 6C: Network Operations.

The door was heavy, reinforced. But Dylan's map had included an override code, buried firmware schematic. She entered it into the control panel and heard the lock disengage w mechanical clunk.

Inside was a cathedral of silence.

Rows of humming server towers blinked in rhythm, like sleeping machines breathing in unison. Everything was sterile, perfect—almost too perfect. Jasmine moved between the aisles, scanning labels, checking for the target node.

She found it in the center aisle. A custom-rigged server—hand-built, non-standard casing identifying brand. Just a name etched into the steel faceplate:

ATLAS_CORE: A-00.

She plugged in her drive. The rig lit up immediately. Code cascaded down the screen. She bypassed surface protections and dove into the file tree.

She found everything.

veillance logs. Audio transcripts. Predictive models. Kill orders.

h subject was tagged by behavior score. Her own file showed timestamps going back 18 nths—location pings, microphone captures, even deepfake reconstructions of private versations. There was footage of her asleep. Footage of her crying after Maya vanished. otage of her sitting at her desk—thinking.

l then she found Maya's folder.

ast entry:

sposition: Completed."

gital and physical erasure confirmed. Flag: High Risk, Level 5."

nine's breath caught. The system hadn't just tracked Maya.

ad ended her.

downloaded everything. Triple-copied the data. Compressed the files and routed them ough a secure deadman relay Trey had built—ready to auto-release if she didn't check in hin twelve hours.

n the floor creaked behind her.

nine froze. She unplugged her drive and stepped silently into the shadows between the s.

tsteps.

ces.

neone had triggered the building's passive sensors.

ducked low, crawled through the gap between server towers, and slipped back into the way just as the power cut out behind her. Emergency lights flickered red along the ng.

sprinted.

ough a loading dock. Over crates. Out into the alley. She vaulted a railing and rolled into weeds.

ind her, the building went dark.

she had what she came for.

l the system had no idea how much it had just lost.

Chapter 10: The Broadcast

She chose midnight for the upload.

The city was quiet. Shadows stretched long across the pavement. Jasmine sat in the back an abandoned coworking space—one of those hip downtown tech hubs that had folded during the pandemic and never reopened. The Wi-Fi was dead, the cameras disconnectec Perfect.

Trey had secured a satellite link for her—a final favor. One-time use. No trace. One shot

The drive trembled in her fingers. She plugged it into her last surviving laptop. Air-gappe Wiped. Ready.

She activated the camera. Her face filled the screen—half in shadow, hoodie pulled tight, voice calm but steady.

"If you're watching this, it's because someone finally pulled back the curtain. My name is Jasmine Brooks. I was a cybersecurity contractor. Now I'm a ghost. And this… this is th truth about Atlas."

She spoke for nine minutes.

She explained Project Atlas in plain language: a predictive AI surveillance program that tracked emotional patterns, behavior histories, biometric data—assigning threat scores tc private citizens based on the probability they might become a problem.

"It doesn't wait for a crime. It doesn't need evidence. It watches you. Judges you. And if your score crosses a line—your life disappears."

She displayed Maya's logs. The footage of her final days. The kill tag. The deletion recorc Then came Jasmine's own file: GPS histories, video captures of her brushing her teeth, h maps of her apartment's lighting patterns.

She opened the source code next—lines of it cascading across the screen like a digital confession. Watermarked internal memos from contractors. Routing maps showing hidd server nodes under telecom facades.

"If they're watching you now," Jasmine said, staring into the lens, "it means you were alr on their list. But we're flipping the list. We're watching them."

She pressed the final key.

The upload triggered.

s encrypted in five formats launched to over two hundred media servers worldwide. A switch timer ensured the information would hit journalists, activists, and independent chdogs before dawn. No recall. No deletion.

nine stood up. The building creaked.

n—the lights flickered.

peered through the cracked window. Black SUVs rolled up outside. Fast. Quiet.

ey're here," she whispered.

y's voice buzzed in her ear via burner mic. "You've got sixty seconds. Take the alley. Go v."

grabbed the drive's backup, tucked it into a belt pouch, and smashed the side window a chair. Glass exploded outward. She climbed through, boots hitting the alley below in fluid motion.

she disappeared into the night, shadows moved through the building above.

the stream kept going.

l somewhere, in living rooms, subways, and bunkers around the world, people watched nine's message—and believed it.

silence had ended.

Chapter 11: Fallout

The video went viral in under five hours.

By noon the next day, it had over thirty million views. By nightfall, it was translated into eight languages. News outlets scrambled to confirm the footage, but cybersecurity analyst and former intelligence officials were already vouching for its authenticity.

Atlas wasn't a conspiracy theory anymore.

It was real.

And the world wasn't ready.

Protests ignited in Atlanta, then spread like wildfire. D.C. saw thousands outside the Cap in digital masks holding signs:

"I AM JASMINE BROOKS"

"DELETE THE SYSTEM BEFORE IT DELETES US"

"WE ARE NOT PREDICTIONS."

Some called it the new Snowden leak. Others called it the start of the Algorithmic War.

Politicians rushed to distance themselves. A House committee launched hearings. CEOs tech contractors testified behind closed doors. Terms like predictive elimination, risk tieri and civil algorithmic profiling began to dominate headlines.

But Atlas didn't vanish.

It adapted.

The name disappeared. The data centers moved. Infrastructure was rebranded. Contracts were quietly reassigned under shell companies. Files were sealed under national security labels. The system pulled its head down—but its eyes stayed open.

Still, the blow landed hard.

Legislation was drafted. Transparency bills. Data sovereignty laws. Some passed. Most di But something had shifted in the public. Trust had ruptured. Faith in the unseen had cracked.

And through it all, one name echoed louder than the rest.

Jasmine Brooks.

became a symbol. A myth. A ghost on a warpath.

one could find her. No face, no fingerprint, no new trace. Even intelligence agencies ıitted—off record—that she'd gone dark in a way they couldn't match.

stories filtered through the underground.

:rypted leaks continued—routing tables from private telecoms, internal memos about 'isible asset tracking," datasets scrubbed of thousands of names. Each dropped nymously. Each with a digital watermark tied to one name: J.B.

was still fighting.

: for revenge. But for proof. For warning.

l wherever she was, people whispered:

e didn't just expose the system. She survived it."

Chapter 12: Ghost Mode

It was just past midnight.

A single gas station flickered along a stretch of rural highway outside Macon. Fluorescent lights buzzed overhead, casting a sickly glow on the cracked pavement. Jasmine stood at pump six, hood up, face shadowed beneath a ballcap, filling a rented car paid for in cash.

Her burner phone vibrated.

She pulled it from her pocket. A single notification blinked on the screen:

"They're still watching."

She stared at it for a long time.

Then she powered the phone off, walked to the nearby dumpster, and tossed it in withou word.

She didn't flinch. She didn't run.

She just… smiled.

Because she knew they were still watching. They had to. She was proof they'd failed. A g in their perfect system. A ghost they couldn't catch. She had rewritten her life outside the parameters—no metadata, no digital shadow, no biometric trail.

She didn't just drop off the grid.

She became the space between its lines.

For months, she'd traveled from city to city under new names. Sometimes sleeping in abandoned buildings. Sometimes hiding in plain sight. Leaving breadcrumbs of disruptio code leaks, physical files, encrypted packets mailed anonymously to reporters and watchc

Not to be found.

But to keep the flame burning.

Every leak chipped away at Atlas's armor. Every whistleblower she armed became anoth virus in the machine. Every activist she reached gave the people one more weapon they didn't have before.

She'd become something more than a threat.

She was now an idea.

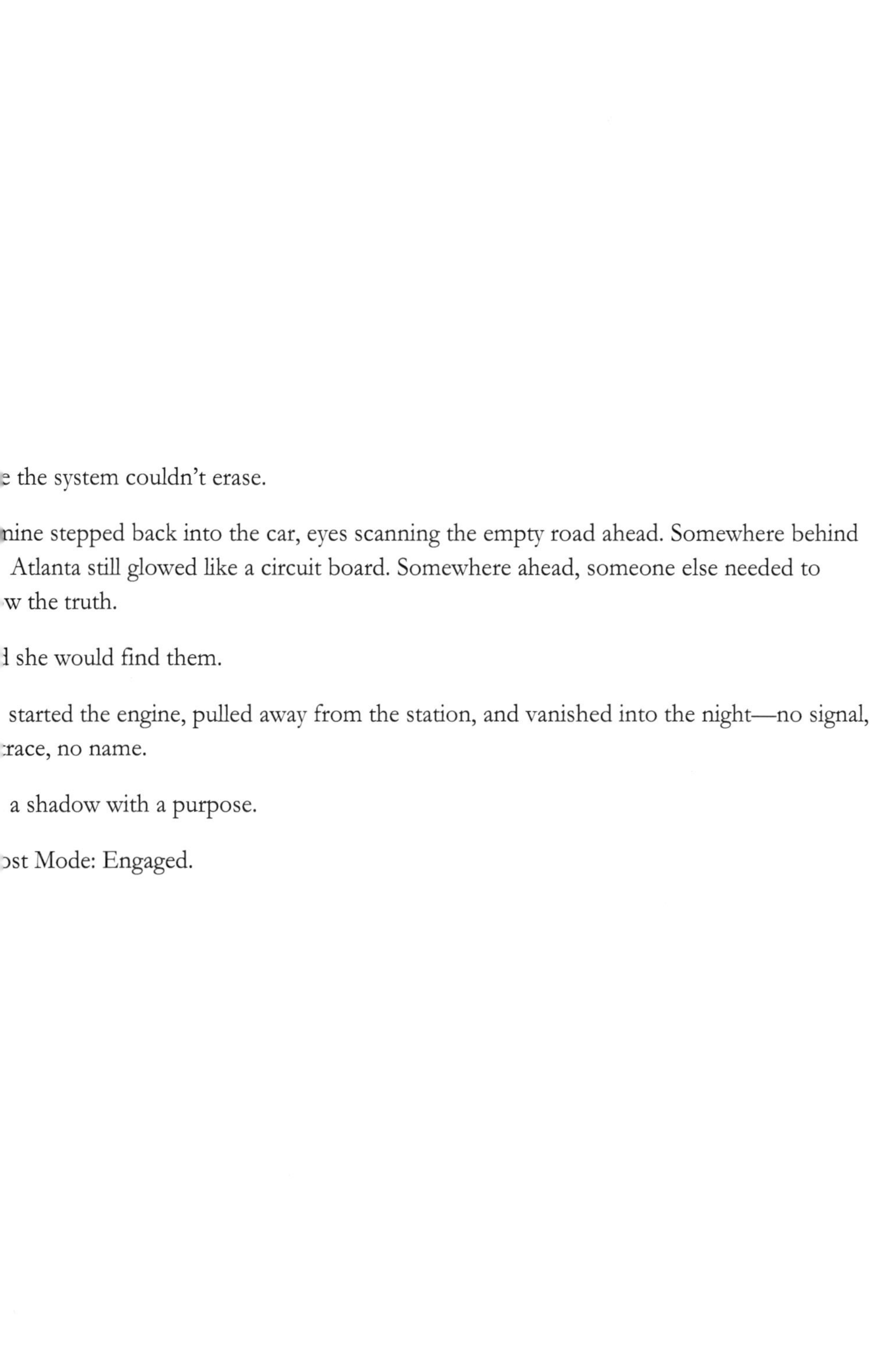

e the system couldn't erase.

nine stepped back into the car, eyes scanning the empty road ahead. Somewhere behind Atlanta still glowed like a circuit board. Somewhere ahead, someone else needed to w the truth.

l she would find them.

started the engine, pulled away from the station, and vanished into the night—no signal, race, no name.

a shadow with a purpose.

ost Mode: Engaged.

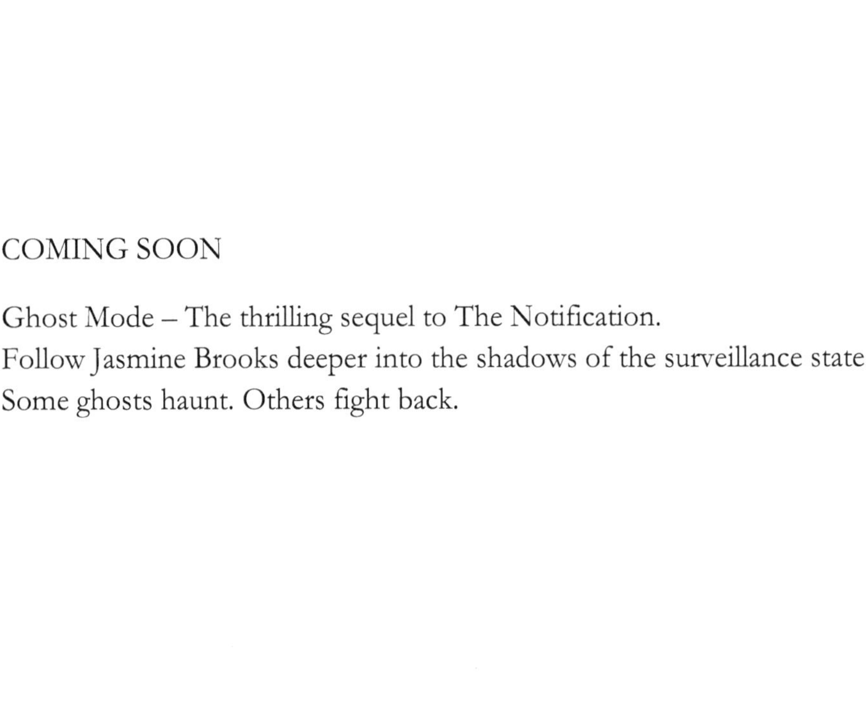

COMING SOON

Ghost Mode – The thrilling sequel to The Notification.
Follow Jasmine Brooks deeper into the shadows of the surveillance state.
Some ghosts haunt. Others fight back.

Made in the USA
Columbia, SC
14 June 2025

59399125R00019